Dear sam
lot's c
~~mum~~ meg POP DILYS
and Judith

NORMAN PRICE

BELLA LASAGNE

JAMES

SARAH

TITLES AVAILABLE IN BUZZ BOOKS

First published 1990 by Buzz Books,
an imprint of the Octopus Publishing Group,
Michelin House, 81 Fulham Road, London, SW3 6RB.

LONDON MELBOURNE AUCKLAND

Fireman Sam © 1985 Prism Art & Design Ltd

Text © 1990 William Heinemann Ltd

Illustrations © 1990 William Heinemann Ltd
Story by Caroline Hill-Trevor
Illustrations by CLIC
Based on the animation series produced by Bumper Films for
S4C/Channel 4 Wales and Prism Art & Design Ltd.
Original idea by Dave Gingell and Dave Jones, assisted by
Mike Young. Characters created by Rob Lee.

ISBN 1 85591 008 X

Printed and bound in the UK by BPCC Paulton Books Ltd.

TREVOR'S TRIAL RUN

Story by Caroline Hill-Trevor
Illustrations by CLIC!

It was the day of the Fire Station Fun Run
and Trevor Evans was on his way to
Pontypandy, dressed in his tracksuit and
trainers, ready to join in. "I wish I was
fitter," he thought, rubbing his stomach.
"It's all the lovely lasagne Bella cooks that's
done it. Never mind, two miles isn't very
far. I should just manage it."

Trevor was so busy thinking about the
run that he didn't notice the oil warning
light flashing in front of him – something
was seriously wrong with his bus.

As Trevor turned the corner into Pandy Lane the bus started hiccupping and making a terrible noise and very soon it stopped altogether.

"Oh bother!" sighed Trevor, suddenly noticing the red light. "It looks as if we're out of oil," and he got out to have a look.

8

"Help!" he cried, grabbing hold of the door to save himself. "The road's all slippery and there's been no rain – it must be oil."

Just as he was wondering what to do next, Trevor heard the sound of an engine.

"That's a bit of luck," he thought. "If I can get a lift into Pontypandy I'll still be in time for the run."

Trevor was standing at the side of the road waving his handkerchief when Fireman Sam and Fireman Elvis Cridlington came round the corner in Jupiter, on their way back to the fire station after a call.

"There's someone waving," said
Fireman Sam, slowing down. "Looks like
Trevor, we'd better stop and help." But as
he braked, Jupiter's tyres slid on the oily
road and they started to skid.

"Watch out, Trevor," cried Elvis, closing
his eyes as they skidded across the road,

narrowly missing the bus. There was a thud
and Jupiter came to a halt.

"You can open your eyes now, Elvis,"
said Fireman Sam. "There's no harm done,
but I think we're stuck in the ditch. I didn't
know the lane was so slippery. Come on,
let's get out."

Pale and shaken, Elvis and Fireman Sam climbed out of Jupiter and had a look around. "Phew, that was a near miss!" said Trevor, mopping his brow with his handkerchief. "For a moment I thought you were going to crash into my bus, and me, for that matter. You wouldn't think oil could cause a skid like that, would you?"

"What's going on here, Trevor?" said Fireman Sam. "Why is there oil all over the road? It's very dangerous you know. Now we'll have to pull Jupiter out of the ditch."

14

Trevor explained what had happened. "A right pair of engines we've got," grumbled Elvis, "one in the ditch and the other broken down. We need help, but hardly anyone comes down this little lane."

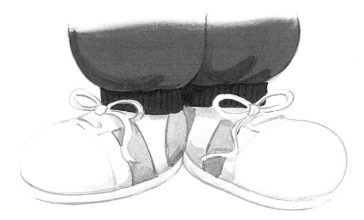

"I'm afraid three firemen are going to miss the Fire Station Fun Run then," added Fireman Sam, looking at the ground gloomily. But then he noticed Trevor's trainers. "Unless," he thought . . .

"Why didn't we think of it before?" said
Fireman Sam, looking up. "Trevor, you're
dressed for running. If you run back up the
lane to the call box and ring the fire station
we'll be out of here in no time."

"I suppose I could," mumbled Trevor, not
looking very happy about the idea.

18

"You'll have to," said Elvis, "after all, if it wasn't for you, Jupiter wouldn't be stuck in the ditch."

"Well, I don't know about that," said Trevor indignantly.

"Off you go, Trevor, at once," repeated Fireman Sam firmly.

"Maybe I'm fitter than I thought," said
Trevor to himself as he jogged slowly up the
road to the call box, breathing deeply.
"I must have run at least a mile by now and
I'm barely out of breath."

20

Feeling more confident he ran on a bit faster, counting to himself, "One-two, one-two, come on now, Trevor, this is easy." A few minutes later he arrived at the 'phone box and went inside.

He lifted the receiver but there was no
sound – the line was dead. "Oh no, the
'phone's out of order! Now what am I going
to do?" he wailed. "There's no point in
going back, I'll have to run on, all the way
to Pontypandy. And if I'm not quick the run
will start without us."

22

He set off again, going as fast as he could,
but getting slower and slower the further he
went. "Can't be much further, surely," he
gasped, beginning to get a stitch. "Must be
round the next corner," he hoped, but there
were quite a few more corners before he
finally saw the Pontypandy church spire.

When Trevor finally arrived in
Pontypandy, Sarah, James, Norman Price
and Station Officer Steele were in the park,
waiting to start the run. Dilys and Bella
were watching proudly.

"Where have you been, Trevor, and
what's happened to your bus, and Fireman
Sam and Elvis, for that matter?" said
Station Officer Steele, looking around.
"Trying to get out of the run, are they?"

Breathlessly, Trevor explained what had happened.

"Never mind," said Station Officer Steele. "Our route takes us up Pandy Lane anyway. There are enough of us here to pull Jupiter out of the ditch. Grab a rope, Trevor! We're waiting to start."

They all lined up. "Uno, due, tre, away you go!" cried Bella, and the fun run started. Following Station Officer Steele, Sarah, James and Norman raced off towards Pandy Lane, with Trevor puffing along behind, carrying the heavy rope.

"Come on, Trevor," Dilys laughed. "You've been eating too much lasagne!"

"Thanks very much, Trevor," grinned
Fireman Sam, when the group reached him.
They attached the rope and with everyone
pulling together, and Elvis revving the
engine, Jupiter came out of the ditch easily.

"We'd better get the road cleaned up,"
said Fireman Sam. "We don't want any
more accidents."

"Wait, Trevor," said Station Officer Steele,
as Trevor climbed into his bus. "Collect the
bus later, you mustn't miss the fun run."

"I think I've done enough running for one day, Sir," sighed Trevor.

"Nonsense, that was just a trial run and, besides, you could do with the practice! Come along now, one-two, one-two . . ."

FIREMAN SAM

STATION OFFICER
STEELE

TREVOR EVANS

ELVIS
CRIDLINGTON